PINGU and His Friends

BBC BOOKS

Pingo couldn't wait to show Pingu his new skis. "They are very smart!" said Pingu, looking at them admiringly.

"Let's go and try them out," said Pingo. "If you get on behind me, we'll get there faster. Hold on tight!"

Along the way, they came across an old barrel. "I've got an idea," said Pingu. "I'll make myself a pair of skis, too."

Pingu sets to work straight away. "These small planks will do – even if they do curve a bit," he said.

"I don't think you'll get far on those skis," warned Pingo. But Pingu had already set off up the hill. Pingo followed him to the top.

"Copy me," he said, "and you'll find it is not at all difficult. The important thing is always to keep your balance."

Pingu had trouble keeping his skis straight and Pingo was already waiting at the bottom of the slope as Pingu slid *slowly* downhill.

"You don't know what fun you're missing!" said Pingo to his friend. "Let me show you." Pingu watched full of admiration.

But Pingo went too fast and didn't notice a dangerous dip in the snow at the bottom of the slope. Luckily, he was not hurt. But, one of his beautiful new skis was broken in two!

"I have to be careful not to fall!" Pingu thought to himself, as he slowly made his way down to help Pingo. "I don't understand why people think this is fun. It seems more like hard work to me."

Pingo tried to warn his friend about the dangerous spot as he approached the bottom of the slope. But it was too late...

CRASH! Pingu fell, just like his friend! "I warned you," laughed Pingo. "Now look what's happened. You've got only one ski, too!"

"Well, at least we each still have one good ski," said Pingo. Putting on one ski each, the two friends snow-scooted happily back to the village together.

A SLEDGE OUTING

Pingo and Ping came to call for Pingu. "We're going sledging. Are you coming, too?" they asked. "We are going to climb that hill."

It was quite a difficult climb, but at last the three friends reached the top.

"You go down faster on your tummy," said Pingo. "No, you don't. It's better on your back," said Ping.

Pingo and Ping shot off down the slope. Pingu tried to follow his friends, but he found that his sledge would hardly move.

Pingo and Ping were waiting for Pingu at the bottom of the hill.
"What's wrong?" they called.

"I think the runners must be rusty," said Pingu.
"I haven't used my sledge for ages."
Ping gave him a rag and some wax to clean the runners.

Ping got rid of the rust and put some wax on the runners.
"I'm ready!" he called. "Let's have a race."

They quickly climbed to the top of the slope and then, one, two, three... They're off! Pingu streaked into the lead.

Pingu's sledge hit a block of ice and broke into small pieces. Poor Pingu was thrown off down the slope – right into the big snowman at the foot of the hill!

"Pingu! Pingu! Where are you?" called his friends, running up. But, Pingu was *inside* the snowman and couldn't answer.

Luckily, Pingo had an idea. The two friends loaded the snowman on to a sledge and took it home.

Once home, they put the snowman in front of the stove and slowly it began to melt.

Bit by bit, a grinning Pingu emerged, rather wet but quite unharmed. The three friends laughed and laughed at their extraordinary adventure.

PINGA GETS LOST

"I've got a lot to do today, Pingu," said his mum. "Will you take your sister with you when you go out to play? Be sure not to come home late."

Pingu met his friend, Pingo, in the park. "Shall we play leapfrog?" suggested Pingo.
"I want to play too!" said Pinga.
"You're too little," said Pingu.

But Pinga insisted and eventually they let her join in. Soon all three of them grew bored of the game. "Let's have a sliding race now," said Pingu.

Pinga sat on the sledge, watching them as
they began sliding along the track.

Pingu and Pingo had such a good time, they forgot all about Pinga and were soon a very long way from the sledge. By the time they returned, the sledge was empty. Pinga had disappeared!

"Pinga, Pinga!" they called as they searched for her everywhere. But, Pinga was nowhere to be found.

"We've got to find her!" cried Pingu. "How can I possibly go home without my little sister?"

By now it was beginning to get dark. Suddenly Pingu saw Pinga's red scarf and a trail of small footprints, leading into a deep, dark crevasse!

"Oh no!" sobbed Pingu. Pingo shouted into the crevasse. "Pinga, Pinga! Are you there? Answer me! Please!"
There was no reply.

"Pingu, we must run and tell your parents straight away," said Pingo.
It was very late by now, as the two dejected little penguins made their way back to the village.

Pingu and Pingo were in tears as Pingu's mum opened the door.

"Mum, we've lost Pinga," sobbed Pingu, hardly able to speak.

"Nonsense!" said his mum. "She's having her supper. Come inside and look."
Pingu and Pingo couldn't believe their eyes.

Pingu was furious. He ran at her shouting. "We've been out there looking for you all afternoon. And all the time you've been here!" "You were to blame too," scolded his mum. "You should have looked after her better."

Pingu felt ashamed, but one thing was certain, and that was that he would certainly look after his sister better in future.

Published by BBC Books, a division of BBC Enterprises Limited, Woodlands, 80 Wood Lane, London W12 OTT
First published 1990. Reprinted 1993 three times. Illustrations by Tony Wolf. Original text by Sibylle von Flüe.

ISBN 0 563 36743 1
Printed and bound in Great Britain by Cambus Litho Ltd, East Kilbride